PUBLIC ENEMY

PUBLIC ENEMY

KENNETH BRANAGH

faber and faber

LONDON · BOSTON

First published in 1988
by Faber and Faber Limited
3 Queen Square London WC1N 3AU

Printed in Great Britain by
Cox & Wyman Ltd Reading Berkshire
All rights reserved

British Library Cataloguing in Publication Data

Branagh, Kenneth
Public enemy.
I. Title
822'.914   PR6052.R41/

ISBN 0-571-15103-5

To Frances and William Branagh

INTRODUCTION

In September 1985 I played the young D. H. Lawrence in a television film. Researching the role I re-read a marvellous volume of Lawrence's letters covering the years between his sixteenth and twenty-seventh birthdays, and the insight it gave me into the working of Lawrence's genius encouraged me to try and develop an idea which had absorbed me for some time. I began writing the first draft of *Public Enemy*.

Rushed off in a splurge of hope and panic that first version none the less contained all the elements of the final play – the effects of long-term unemployment, neo-gangster life, personal obsession, the insidious power of the screen – but it lacked coherence and the essential American movie/Belfast metaphor was unbalanced.

The play was put away in a drawer, and remained there for a year, to be read only by a few close friends, amongst them a writer, an actor and a director, whose comments were carefully recorded in readiness for the next attempt.

In the autumn of '86 Peter James, Artistic Director of the Lyric Theatre, Hammersmith, read this first draft and agreed to a co-production of the play with the Renaissance Theatre Company, which I had recently founded with David Parfitt. With production dates fixed I had no choice but to return to the script. At this point I was blessed in our appointment of the director, Malcolm McKay. A writer himself he understood immediately my anxieties as a first-time playwright. We discussed the flaws of my first draft, how to re-work the material, and over the two subsequent versions he provided the confidence and expertise needed to give my ideas theatrical reality.

By the time rehearsals began we had decided on several fundamentals. First, the play was *not* a fantasy. The Belfast we would create had to be grittily real if the play was going to work. Whatever Tommy Black achieved by way of costumes, tricks and stunts in his stage show had to be what a real Belfast boy could have managed. The bars, the street, the Blacks' house all had to bear the stamp of the *real* place, not a screen version. To this end Geoff Rose, our designer, produced a marvellous reconstruction of a Belfast street corner. But in the height and shape of its walls, his design was at the same time suggestive of some alternative cityscape in silhouette, and this ambiguity was tremendously useful in shifting the audience's perceptions at climactic moments like the 'shoot-out' where we seem to cross over into film-land Chicago, *knowing* ourselves to be in a real 1980s Belfast.

Three interchangeable trucks emerged from sliding garage-like doors in the middle of this street-corner set. Each one of these – the bar, Kitty's house, the Blacks' sitting room – was lit to give an immediate indoors effect, while the rest of the set remained dark, thus solving the problem of the different locations. The sliding doors and set trucks were also part of that solution. We knew that any production of the play had to move as swiftly and smoothly as a movie and many design decisions were made with that end in mind. Scene changes became cinematic – rapid, dramatic advances of the action, brief but inherently exciting.

This theatrical style suited exactly the character of the piece. Without sacrificing the reality of the place and people we wanted the audience's sense of our story to correspond to the way in which the characters see (or rather wish to see) their own lives – fast-moving, dramatic, heroic. Music was vital in this; scene endings were often marked musically and almost all links between scenes were accompanied by a driving, dramatic score – the music of Belfast in the 1980s but, again, suggestive of the soundtracks of gangster films (though we also used effects that were specifically 'Belfast' – soldiers with walkie-talkies, children's rhymes, drunks shouting).

A major problem was the character of Tommy Black. We were determined that the role should not simply be a showy actor's vehicle, and in the first half anyone attempting it should avoid lapsing into 'Cagney' unless specifically directed to do so in the script. Tommy's Belfast street talk and his Chicago film-land equivalent with its rat-a-tat quick-fire irony should remain distinct until the moment Tommy Black becomes a killer. Then the Cagney persona, with its full-blown Americanisms, bravura confidence and brash morality finally takes over, the outward demonstration of the crazed heroism inside Tommy Black.

The character of Thompson is more open to individual

interpretation. In our production we saw him moving dreamer-like on the fringes of the action. In Act Two, Scene Thirty-six he did not in fact join Ma in the 'Blacks' set but played to her, as if re-enacting a scene from his memory. He was always an observer, unable to interact with other people. We even thought about leaving him on stage throughout, though in the end he did occasionally exit after certain scenes.

I think that any group working on the play should bring their own vision of it to bear, just as our company did. Certainly our version achieved its distinct character as much through the work of the actors, director, designers – everyone taking part – as through me. For that reason this text remains as clean of direction as it can be. The words and ideas can then be freshly re-examined without being confused by a prompt-copy record of what we did. To readers and potential producers I would add that though they're fascinating, you don't have to see the films *Public Enemy*, *White Heat*, or *Angels with Dirty Faces* to understand this play. In fact, that might encourage you to see the play as a fantasy after all, which it isn't. Nothing that happens in this play would be impossible in Belfast, or anywhere else, today.

KENNETH BRANAGH

CHARACTERS

THOMPSON
TOMMY BLACK
DAVEY BOYD
GEORGE PEARSON
CHARLIE HARPER (pianist)
KITTY ROGERS
MA
ROBERT BLACK
KEVIN O'DONNELL

Public Enemy was first performed at the Lyric, Hammersmith, on 15 July 1987 by the Renaissance Theatre Company. The cast was as follows:

THOMPSON	John Rogan
TOMMY BLACK	Kenneth Branagh
DAVEY BOYD	Gerard Horan
GEORGE PEARSON	George Shane
CHARLIE HARPER	Derek Crewe
KITTY ROGERS	Ethna Roddy
MA	Brenda Peters
ROBERT BLACK	Fabian Cartwright
KEVIN O'DONNELL	Derek Crewe
Director	Malcom McKay
Producer	David Parfitt
Design	Geoff Rose
Lighting	Kevin Sleep
Fights	Nick Hall
Choreography	Julie Fell
Sound	Tristan Bickerton

ACT ONE

SCENE ONE

Darkness. Music. A faint tap, tap, tap.

THOMPSON: One guy.
    One dream.
    Maybe the wrong time.
    Maybe the wrong place.
    Who knows? Maybe.
    But life don't live in 'maybes'.
    The kid knew that.
    The kid knew it all.
    (*The music swells.*)

SCENE TWO

A Protestant bar and social club, Belfast. TOMMY BLACK *is taking part in a talent contest, impersonating James Cagney in* Yankee Doodle Dandy.

TOMMY BLACK: (Sings:) I'm a Yankee Doodle Dandy,
    Yankee Doodle Do or Die,
    A real live nephew of my uncle Sam,
    Born of the Fourth of July.

    I've got a Yankee Doodle Sweetheart,
    She's my Yankee Doodle joy,
    Yankee Doodle came to London
    Just to ride the ponies;
    I am that Yankee Doodle boy.
    (*Dances.*)
    Yankee Doodle came to London,
    Just to ride the ponies,
    I am that Yankee Doodle boy.
    (*The music stops.*)

I

SCENE THREE

The club. Applause and music continue faintly. TOMMY *is joined by his friend* DAVEY.

DAVEY: That was wonderful, George. I know we've got a great success on our hands.

TOMMY: Easy there. That's only the first act. The critics might have left already. Don't go countin' on anything.

DAVEY: Don't worry, George. Don't worry about a thing. You can feel it in the air, can't you? Nothing can touch you when that feeling's in the air.

SCENE FOUR

THOMPSON: Any they sure couldn't touch him that night.
Nobody could.
The kid was on his way.
He took 'em all in.
No sweat. No strain.
Everybody on his side.
Everybody in the same dream.

SCENE FIVE

The club. Enter PEARSON, *an Ulsterman. He carries a microphone.*

PEARSON: Hey, you two! Over here!

THOMPSON: (*Ulster*) Well, maybe not everybody.
Just yet.
The dreaming has to stop sometimes,
For all of us.

(TOMMY *and* DAVEY *join* PEARSON.)

PEARSON: One number, Black. That's what I told you. That's what I meant. None of this bloody nonsense. I can disqualify you, you know.

DAVEY: I've nothin' to do with it, Geordie. I didn't know it was against the rules.

PEARSON: Well, your great mate did.

DAVEY: Well, c'mon and sit down. Have a wee drink and we'll sort it out.

TOMMY: Now listen here. Nobody brings the curtain down on a George M. Cohan song.

PEARSON: Don't try makin' a fool of me, son.

DAVEY: Give it a rest, Tommy.

PEARSON: What's your bloody game, Black –

TOMMY: (*To the audience in his own natural Belfast accent*) Listen, folks. Listen. If I could just have a moment of your time. I have one quick thank you to say. Geordie Pearson here's put a hell of a lot of work into organizing this contest and I just wanted to say thanks very much and I hope he didn't mind me puttin' in that wee extra bit from *Yankee Doodle Dandy*, with my good friend Davey Boyd, just to round off the number. Anyway enough's enough. Thanks for watchin' and I'll hand you back to the man of the moment. (*Passing the microphone back*) There you are, Geordie. (*Cagney*) You dirty rat.

(*Laughter. As he exits he shouts to the audience:*)
He never even said that!

PEARSON: Right. That was Thomas Black there . . . and . . . right. Er, anyway, short break now, folks. Don't forget to buy your raffle tickets from Big John at the bar there. Remember we've one more act to go and then it's up to you to decide who's the overall winner. Thanks.

THOMPSON: I'd have said there was no contest.
      That kid had something special.
      Guts, if nothin' else to risk crossin' Geordie Pearson.

PEARSON: Tell your mate I wanna see him. Now.

DAVEY: I'll try and find him, Geordie.

PEARSON: Make sure you do or he's out of this contest.

THOMPSON: Well, they didn't report that bit, Geordie.
      Not in the paper I read.
      What there was was easily missed.
      Not by me. But by some.
      Some people skim through the paper, others maybe just turn to the TV or the sport. Not me.

3

I *scour* the thing.
Professional discipline of course.
Years of that.
Too many.
But even so. I'm still a good copper.
Was.
I'd always tried to look further than anyone else.
Read the signs early for trouble. Be ahead of myself.
Be ahead of everyone.
Be good.
Know what I mean?

PEARSON: Where the hell's he gone?

THOMPSON: Well. I knew something was brewin'. You get a
strong nose in this job. Good instinct. You have to in this
town, in this job or you're dead. Simple as that.
There was something goin' on. Outside of me or inside of
me. Maybe both.
But this place was changin'. Had to. So was this job. That
had to happen as well.
So I kept lookin'. Lookin' for the wee things.
The harmless things.
You'll learn more from that than your boss – whoever he is
this week – army, police, government – whatever.
Well, maybe I'd find nothin', but I picked up some local
colour all right, including on that fateful night the news
that James Cagney was alive and well and performin' in a
wee hall in Belfast.

'An uncanny reincarnation of the great man in his finest
musical triumph. Young Thomas Black's ingenuity and
commitment to the impersonation should be saluted.'

Commitment. That's what the paper said. And that was a
word with which I had a fast-fading relationship. Well,
Tommy Black threw it right back at me.

Ridiculous it may have been. Bizarre. But it made me
smile. And I thought 'Good for you, Thomas Black in

your wee hall in Belfast'.
Bit of commitment.
Maybe I could learn somethin' from that.
Maybe I did.

SCENE SIX

The club. KITTY *is midway through her act.*
KITTY: (*Sings:*) Sometimes it's hard to be a woman,
    Givin' all your love to just one man,
    But if you love him,
    Then be proud of him,
    Cos after all he's just a man.

    Stand by your man,
    Give him two arms to cling to,
    And something warm to sing to
    When nights are cold and lonely.

    Stand by your man,
    And show the world you love him
    And give him all the love you can.
    Stand by your man.
  (*Applause.*)

SCENE SEVEN

The club. TOMMY *and* DAVEY *are watching* KITTY *perform.*
TOMMY: Gee, there's one swell dish. I think I'm gonna go for
    her.
DAVEY: What? Are you kiddin'?
TOMMY: C'mon, Matt, you need your ears syringed.
DAVEY: Matt? Who am I this time?
TOMMY: Who *are* you? Why do I bother talking? I'm always
    alone when I'm with Matt.
DAVEY: You've had too many ginger beers, haven't you?

TOMMY: You're in the wrong picture, kid. We gotta sharpen you up, muttonhead.

DAVEY: Ay, well, when you're at it check yourself out. If you spoke English part of the time that would help. I think this performin' lark's gone straight to your head.

TOMMY: So what about the broad, Dave?

(*Pause.*)

THOMPSON: Like I said, the kid got everybody goin'.

DAVEY: Well, you're so bloody persistent – (*Picking up on* TOMMY's *accent*) I'd say the broad's pretty tasty under all dat dressin' up stuff. I'd also say de broad's pretty good, so she's gonna run you close at the finish. And for wraps I'd say dat de broad's real class, right? And she ain't gonna take nuthin' from no two-bit heel like you, OK?

TOMMY: Movin' in on me, shmuck, huh?

DAVEY: Maybe I am, kid. Maybe I am.

TOMMY: That's not bad you know, Dave.

DAVEY: I know. Christ, I should have entered the bloody contest myself.

TOMMY: Dat ain't in *my* script, kid.

DAVEY: Hey! Straighten your tie, fella. It's decision time.

SCENE EIGHT

The club.

PEARSON: If I could have your attention, folks. Thanks very much. Now the judges have had a very hard time here tonight and they've asked me to thank all the contestants for the hard work they've put in. It's a credit to the neighbourhood. Well done to you all. But anyway a decision had to be made and this is what the judges have come up with. In second place for 'Standing by her man' very well indeed (and who *wouldn't* wanna have her standin' by you), Miss Kitty Rogers. Come on up, Kitty.

(*She arrives on stage.*)

Well done, love. Some of us thought you should have been

6

first, but never mind. The winner of tonight's talent contest for his 'astonishing' portrayal of James Cagney's 'Yankee Doodle Dandy' is Mr Thomas Black.
(*Applause.*)

TOMMY: Thank you, ladies and gentlemen. You know this means a great deal to me. I know that some might say I've been on the road too long. Well, who knows? Like all of us I've had some good times and some bad times. But it isn't every family that gets to dance together every day –

PEARSON: Don't start that crap –

TOMMY: – but I just wanna say that now I *am* here, I'm just proud that my Ma could watch me tonight. And I know that somewhere up there Papa's watching too. . .

PEARSON: Now listen, son. . .

THOMPSON: Give him a break, Geordie. Remember his oul man . .

PEARSON: If you're takin' the piss. . .

TOMMY: And I know that Papa would want me to receive this in the way the Cohans always have. Ladies and gentlemen, my mother thanks you, my father thanks you, my sister thanks you and I thank you. Good night. (*Then in his Belfast accent*) And I expect oul Geordie Pearson thanks you as well folks! All the best – good night!
(*Applause.*)

PEARSON: Right. There you are, folks. Well, there's a character for you. And there's your winner tonight. Right. We're drawing the raffle in half an hour, don't forget, folks. So have your tickets ready. Here. Black. I wanna talk to you.

TOMMY: Two minutes, Geordie. I'll be right with you.

SCENE NINE

The club. TOMMY *rejoins* DAVEY.

DAVEY: Well done, fella. Hey, you know you've got Pearson ragin'.

TOMMY: What, you think we'll have the UDA bangin' on the door again, eh?

7

DAVEY: For Christ's sake keep your voice down. (*Whispers:*) It
wouldn't surprise me. Look, we may buy him a drink later
on or we might be in trouble.

TOMMY: From that shmuck Putty-Nose?

DAVEY: To hell with his nose. Just watch his mouth and who he
shoots it off to. He's got superiors, you know, and they're a
bloody sight more clever and dangerous than he is – bunch of
cowboys the lot of them.

TOMMY: Not cowboys. Gangsters.

DAVEY: Cowboys, gangsters – what the hell difference does it
make?

TOMMY: It makes all the difference in the world where we're
going.

DAVEY: Who's going where?

TOMMY: Well, you're going to find Pearson now and tell him to
meet us down the club tomorrow lunchtime, so I can buy
him a drink and apologize.

DAVEY: I am not. Are you kiddin', anyway. *You* buy him a drink.
What with? Scotch mist? We all know where your cheque's
gone this week.

TOMMY: I'll find the dough, don't worry. And get a move on.
You'll have to run if you're going to do that and get to
Nelson Street by half-eleven.

DAVEY: What am I going to Nelson Street for?

TOMMY: To meet *me*, stupid.

DAVEY: Why can't you find Pearson and go to Nelson Street on
your own?

TOMMY: Cos dat ain't in de plan, kid. Anyways I gotta make a
play for the broad.

DAVEY: I've told you? You've no hope –

TOMMY: Nelson Street. Half an hour. Get moving.
(*Alone.*)
You got the first round, Tom. Now come on. No slip ups.
No sweat, no strain. Whaddya hear? Whaddya say?

THOMPSON: Geordie Pearson.
> Local loudmouth and small-time hoodlum.
> I guess you got his kind of scum on the mainland.
> But here we legalize it. You join the mob and call it a cause.

> He's small fry, of course.
> Easy to deal with inside.
> So are the guys who *believe*. The ones who know why they're fighting. Same romantic madness in their hearts. Both sides. They know what they want. They just don't know when to stop. It's the Irish way.

> No, it's the hard bastards in the middle you can't suss.
> The godfathers. Hidin' behind banners and pullin' the strings on the Pearsons. They divide the town.
> All for a killin'.
> Money and power.
> And that eats me up. It still does.

> But folk stick it out.
> And a good wee 'do'. A good harmless night out. A talent contest down at your local wee club among your own. It's two fingers to the mobs. It's two fingers to the cops. It says 'life goes on'. And there's no harm in it.
> Ask Tommy Black.

SCENE ELEVEN

The club. TOMMY *joins* KITTY.

TOMMY: Whaddya hear, whaddya say?
KITTY: What do I what, what do I what?
TOMMY: Hey, you crazy mixed-up chick. Can't you understand plain old American/Irish/English?

KITTY: Is that what it is?

TOMMY: Sure. Plain as the nose on that pretty little face.

KITTY: Watch it.

TOMMY: Hey, kid. I know you're sore about losin'.

KITTY: No, I'm not. I thought you were brilliant.

TOMMY: Thanks very much. So why the long face?

KITTY: Nothin'.

TOMMY: Nuthin' don't mean nuthin'. You tell me the truth or I'm gonna fill you so full of lead you could start work as a pencil.

KITTY: (*Garbo*) I vant to be alone.

TOMMY: You certainly do not. What's wrong?

KITTY: I've no money, mister, and I'd better be going.

TOMMY: Stop right there, sweetheart. No dame's gonna run out on Tommy Powers. What would the lady like to drink?

KITTY: I'm not spongin' off anybody and what do you think you'll get if you buy me a drink?

TOMMY: Bit of company, that's all. I'm on me own, so are you. We were the best things in this contest, so there must be something wrong with us. D'ya fancy a bit of a crack and we can work out what it is?

KITTY: I can't buy you one.

TOMMY: You're awful proud.

KITTY: I'm awful broke.

TOMMY: Well, when you can, I'm not bothered.

KITTY: It won't be for a while. I spent this week's cheque on this bloody dress.

TOMMY: On the brew, eh?

KITTY: Ay.

TOMMY: Snap. Mine's went on this bloody suit.

KITTY: Well, where's your money comin' from then?

TOMMY: I know a bloke.

KITTY: What, and he goes out and picks it off the trees, does he?

TOMMY: More or less.

KITTY: I think you're a chancer, mister, but I will have your drink, thanks very much.

(*He signals to the barman.*)

TOMMY: What made you dress in that get-up?

KITTY: You've a bit of a cheek. You're hardly a wall-flower yourself.

TOMMY: But this suits me. You look ridiculous.

KITTY: I don't think I'll have that drink after all.

TOMMY: Hey. I'm only jokin'. It was a great number.

KITTY: Ay, but you're the one with the bottle of whiskey and I'm the one with the drum of Quality Street.

TOMMY: You can give them to your ma.

KITTY: No ma.

TOMMY: Sorry about that. I don't suppose your old man eats sweets?

KITTY: No. That's why I was after the whiskey.

TOMMY: Ay, I see.

KITTY: Do you?

TOMMY: No. Was he in here the night?

KITTY: No. He's not well.

TOMMY: Ach, Jeez, sorry. I'm not meanin' to pry here.

KITTY: You're all right, mister. If you're buying me a drink you can have a wee bit of family history thrown in for nothing.

TOMMY: It's a pity he didn't see you.

KITTY: Ay, it's a pity about a lot of things, isn't it? But I'm buggered if it's gonna get me down. I mean you're right. I do look ridiculous.

TOMMY: No, you don't. No, no.

KITTY: Yes, I do.

TOMMY: Yes, you do. You're right.

KITTY: Well, I don't bloody care, cos I had a good time up there tonight. I really enjoyed it. And you made me laugh yourself. More power to you, I say.

TOMMY: Thanks very much.

KITTY: I'm all for nutcases.

TOMMY: Hey, watch it.

KITTY: Hey. I'm only jokin'. It was a great number.

TOMMY: *Touché*, kid! And cheers. You gonna keep this up then?

KITTY: What – Kitty Rogers sings Country-and-Western classics?

TOMMY: Ay.

KITTY: Catch yourself on.

TOMMY: But something, eh?

KITTY: Oh ay. Something to get me out and about.

TOMMY: It'd stop you worryin' about the oul fella.

KITTY: That's who I'm doing it for really. Well, him and me. If I'd a job. Or if I just did something really well. Something that would please him. Wouldn't matter what. That would be enough. It'll happen.

TOMMY: I'm sure it will, blue eyes, and it'll happen with me.

KITTY: Will it now?

TOMMY: You're meetin' me here tomorrow at one o'clock, right?

KITTY: Wrong.

TOMMY: Right. And we're gonna start havin' some fun in this town, right?

KITTY: Wrong.

TOMMY: Right. And I'm gonna have to go on like this all night before I get a straight answer out of you. Wrong?

KITTY: Right. (*Laughs.*) It's not all that bad, you know, mister. Whoever the hell it is. I'll have to start goin' to the movies, won't I?

TOMMY: You don't have to, kid, from now on you're in them.

KITTY: Oh ay? And the first show's tomorrow at one, is it?

TOMMY: Could be. Go on, canary, get your nose wet.

KITTY: I might be in town and maybe I'll wander in and maybe I won't.

TOMMY: Maybe's a dangerous word.

KITTY: And I'm a dangerous woman.

TOMMY: And this is a dangerous moment. Cos I don't have any money to pay for these drinks.

KITTY: What?

TOMMY: Never trust a stranger, sucker.

KITTY: You wee –

TOMMY: You're all right. We'll make a quiet run for it. You're goin' to the toilet. I'm pickin' up my prize, right – don't look back.

KITTY: My da would kill me if he found out.

TOMMY: He won't know nuthin'. Remember, in here tomorrow at one.

KITTY: I'll see how I feel. See how my da is.

TOMMY: He'll be great. And don't worry about me, kid.
KITTY: I won't. (*She exits*)
TOMMY: Well, I'm sayin' don't, see. I gonna be top of the world.
Right, Ma?

SCENE TWELVE

The Blacks' house. TOMMY *has joined* MA.

MA: Top of the world, that's right, son. Well, you're top of
Belfast tonight, son. No question. I was like Lady Muck
goin' round there.
TOMMY: That's my Ma. And that's one in the eye for Simpson,
right?
MA: Your father would have been proud. I know that. I don't
think it'll make any difference to Simpson one way or
another.
TOMMY: Hey, come on. I told you we ain't talking that way no
more.
MA: Ay, well, it's the truth, son. Like it or not. He wants me out
of that shop and that's all there is to it.
TOMMY: Come on, Ma. You been there longer than any of those
guys. They need you more than –
MA: They do not need me. They've got computers doing things I
can't understand or begin to learn. Even when you're
operatin' the till there's that many new procedures I just get
flustered.
TOMMY: Ma.
MA: He's got me down to no more than a shelf-filler and at my age
I'm not much use for that. I'll be out the first opportunity he
gets. One of the younger ones'll be in to supervise.
TOMMY: They ain't promotin' nobody and you're stayin' put.
MA: Stop your nonsense this once, Tommy. I'm not imagining it
and it's not goin' away.
TOMMY: You could get another job.
MA: Son. Wise up. Look at yourself and your brother. How long?
TOMMY: Long enough.

13

MA: Ay, long enough. And if I take to it like you do, I'll spend the rest of my days in our front room with the blinds drawn.

TOMMY: There's reasons, Ma.

MA: Ay, and I wish to hell I knew them.

TOMMY: All that's behind me now.

MA: I hope so, son. I hope so. I wish your da was here, I know that.

THOMPSON: That would have been better for all of us, Mrs Black.

TOMMY: Or maybe Robert.

MA: Ay well, maybe he was busy, son. You know what he's like. Always out lookin' for work.

TOMMY: Not in the evenings. He could've come.

MA: Ay well, never mind. I was there. And I'm very proud. And a wee bit tipsy.

TOMMY: We're gonna get even, Ma.

MA: Whatever you say, son.

SCENE THIRTEEN

The Blacks' house. Enter ROBERT.

ROBERT: Good evening, Mother. Didn't expect to find you here.

MA: Ay. Well. There you are. How was your day, son?

ROBERT: Not bad. I went to the Adult Education tonight.

MA: Very good. Very good. We're doing a wee bit of celebratin', son.

ROBERT: I'm glad you found the excuse.

MA: But sure you haven't forgotten. Tonight's the night.

ROBERT: What? Oh, the thing. . . ay.

TOMMY: Ay, the thing. The thing you couldn't make it to. And yes, I'm very well, thanks. Yeh, it seemed to go OK. I mean, it's funny you should ask –

ROBERT: Oh, you're with us, are you?

TOMMY: Oh, I'm with you all right, Robert.

MA: Now you two, don't start.

ROBERT: Sorry, Mother.

14

MA: I think you should congratulate your brother.

ROBERT: Why? Is he thinking of leavin' the house durin' daylight?

MA: Tommy won tonight.

ROBERT: Won what?

MA: The talent contest.

ROBERT: Oh, right.

MA: It was great, son. They were all cheering and everything.

ROBERT: How much?

TOMMY: What?

ROBERT: How much did you win?

TOMMY: They weren't cash prizes. I got a bottle of whiskey.

ROBERT: Jesus.

TOMMY: It's a wee club for Christ's sake. What do you expect?

ROBERT: And how much did that get-up cost you?

TOMMY: None of your business.

ROBERT: More than your dole cheque for sure, and I know where the rest came from.

MA: Now, look, boys.

TOMMY: I suppose you think I should be writin' poems and stuff.

ROBERT: What are you talkin' about?

TOMMY: Books and all that stuff don't mean everything.

ROBERT: Christ, have you got one sentence of your own?

MA: Now, give it up the both of yous.

TOMMY: I'm sorry, Ma. I'm sorry, Robert. I know I'm stupid sometimes . . . about things . . . but I do think my own . . . I'm sorry. I just wish you could have been there, mate. Anyway. No harm done. No hard feelings.

ROBERT: No hard feelings, Tom. I'm sorry I missed your little show. I don't hate your play-actin' and makin' fun and that, but we mustn't give up, fella, eh? We mustn't give up.

TOMMY: I don't wanna give up.

ROBERT: Well then, you've gotta get away from that video, haven't you? You've sat in front of it a hell of a long time, you know.

MA: Well, we're all made different, son.

TOMMY: Bob's right, Ma. I did give up. Not any more.

MA: Good. Well, you're a bottle of whiskey better off now.

TOMMY: You bet. What say we break into it right now?

ROBERT: Don't think so, Tom. I've to be up in the morning. I've taken that wee part-time thing, Ma.

MA: OK, son.

TOMMY: You've got a job?

MA: Robert has to go to bed, son. We'll save the winner's whiskey for another time.

TOMMY: Sure thing. Hey, Bob, what are you up to tomorrow night?

ROBERT: Why?

TOMMY: They've got the bowlin' awards here. I got myself booked tonight as the cabaret.

ROBERT: What, this Cagney thing?

TOMMY: Ay.

ROBERT: Well, I'm not sure.

MA: It'd be your chance to make up for tonight.

TOMMY: It'll be a different routine, you see. And I'm getting paid for it.

ROBERT: How much?

TOMMY: Twenty pounds.

MA: That's great, son.

TOMMY: Well, it's a start, Ma. Whaddya say, Bob?

ROBERT: Maybe.

TOMMY: You'll need to be there by nine o'clock, absolute latest.

ROBERT: Can't do it, sorry.

TOMMY: Why the hell not? This once.

MA: Robert.

ROBERT: All right, all right, I'll be there at nine.

TOMMY: Thanks. I appreciate it.

ROBERT: Good night, Ma.

MA: Night, son.

TOMMY: Night, Robert.

ROBERT: See you tomorrow, kid.

TOMMY: I wish he wouldn't call me that.

MA: Ach, you're too sensitive, son.

TOMMY: Ay, maybe. You're right. C'mon, we may get you to bed.

MA: You should be in bed yourself after all that.

16

TOMMY: I think I'll hang on for a bit. Have a wee think.

MA: Well, you know best, son. I'll get young Jim to walk me over the road.

TOMMY: Ay. Ma.

MA: Yes, son.

TOMMY: I need to buy something.

MA: Son, for goodness' sake.

TOMMY: It's a special video.

MA: Why can't you just hire it?

TOMMY: I have to own it, Ma. I just have to. You'll get the money back tomorrow night.

MA: How d'ya know the shop'll have it?

TOMMY: It's ordered.

MA: I don't know why you bother. The films you like are on the TV often enough. Oul rubbish, the lot of them.

TOMMY: Please, Ma.

MA: How much?

TOMMY: Can you manage a tenner?

MA: No, but I'll have to if you're gonna be top of the world, won't I?

TOMMY: That's right, Ma. Now, c'mon, get some shut-eye and walk into Simpson's tomorrow with your head held high, cos your son's the star of the neighbourhood.

MA: All right, you big fool, you. Night.

TOMMY: Night, Ma. (*She exits*) That big brother of yours better be there tomorrow night, right? Or the deal's off. Cos I don't take nuthin' from nobody, see? Right. So you got the alibi – now you get the wheels.

SCENE FOURTEEN

Nelson Street. TOMMY *meets up with* DAVEY.

DAVEY: Where the hell have you been? Must be off my head waitin' here. Anythin' could have happened.

TOMMY: Well, whaddya hear, whaddya say, if that old yellow streak ain't shown up in Matt one more time.

17

DAVEY: Yellow, me arse. I'm waitin' round late at night on a dark street in Belfast for someone who used to be my mate before he lost his marbles.

TOMMY: Who's lost his marbles? Did you see that tonight? Did you see what I did?

DAVEY: Ay, you cocky wee git. And where the hell did you learn to do it? It wasn't bad, you know.

TOMMY: Wasn't bad?

DAVEY: Not as good as my bit, but –

TOMMY: It was bloody brilliant, son. And I'll tell you why.

DAVEY: Who will?

TOMMY: What?

DAVEY: Which one of you will tell me why?

TOMMY: Hey, you're pickin' this up, Dave, aren't you?

DAVEY: Not quick enough, son, but carry on.

TOMMY: There's no carry on to carry on with. I've cracked it, son.

DAVEY: Who's cracked what, I don't want to know; just tell me are you back in circulation or not?

TOMMY: Can't mess you about, Davey, can I?

DAVEY: Not if you want a hand with stupid schemes that nobody else would even think about.

TOMMY: You ain't so dumb, Matt, after all.

DAVEY: No, Jimmy.

TOMMY: Well, I'm tellin' you, we're in the money, kid. You know the press were in tonight.

DAVEY: Ay, the fella who does the wedding reports.

TOMMY: It's a start, but we gotta exploit it. We gotta have pictures.

DAVEY: What for?

TOMMY: Bookings, Davey. Money. A way out of Chicago.

DAVEY: Will I be in these pictures?

TOMMY: I can't do it without you, kid.

DAVEY: My ma always said I was photosthetic.

TOMMY: She was a fine woman. Anyway, one problem.

DAVEY: Maybe I can lend a hand, kid.

TOMMY: That's it, Matt.

DAVEY: Offload some of the booze, huh?

TOMMY: Now we're talking.

DAVEY: Shyst a heist, yeh?

TOMMY: Yeh, shyst a heist.

DAVEY: Broaden a broad.

TOMMY: That's right. But the first thing we need is a gun.

DAVEY: Forget it.

TOMMY: Davey!

DAVEY: What the hell do you need a gun for? Jeezus, we've both spent years trying to stay away from them.

TOMMY: For the pictures, Davey, the pictures. What do people remember? A song-and-dance man and a gangster. We've got to do both. We'll coin it in, but only if we go the whole hog. I've gotta be Jimmy Cagney. You've gotta be the best mate. We need the equipment.

DAVEY: So, where do we go to get them? Down the supermarket? Wise up. Guns are for Geordie Pearson and Co.

TOMMY: Exactly.

DAVEY: What?

TOMMY: Couldn't be easier. Why do you think we're takin' Pearson to lunch tomorrow?

DAVEY: Oh, Christ, Tommy.

TOMMY: Look, he's the biggest mouth there ever was and thick with it. A couple of pints and a bit of brown-nosin' will do it. You've heard him shoutin' his mouth off. We'll know where to get a gun after a session with him. Then we 'borrow' it for half an hour. Do the pictures. Take it straight back. No sweat. No strain. Whaddya hear, whaddya say?

DAVEY: I'll meet Pearson. I'll listen. I'll promise nothin' else.

TOMMY: I just need you to be there, OK? He likes you.

DAVEY: Ay, he likes me, cos I give him tick in the bar when nobody else will.

TOMMY: And you end up payin' for it, right?

DAVEY: Right.

TOMMY: Well, now's your chance for a wee bit of revenge he won't even know about.

DAVEY: You're a canny wee bastard now you're back in the land of the livin', aren't you?

TOMMY: Top of the world, kid, just like I said.

DAVEY: Here, d'ya ever think about leaving Belfast?

TOMMY: Oh, yeh. That's what we're gonna do. You and me both. Sooner than you think.

DAVEY: Well, you'll do for me, Tommy Black.
(*Exits.*)

TOMMY: That's right, Matt. I'll do for you all right.

SCENE FIFTEEN

THOMPSON: So what else was he supposed to do? There could have been worse things than sittin' in watchin' the television. He was certainly Mr Individual. He'd managed to grow up right through the troubles, in the centre of the troubles, and stay clean. His kind of clean. No love lost for the police. Nor the UDA at a time when that could mean big trouble for a Protestant lad and his folk. But he managed. Stood up for himself. Made a name as Mr Outsider and then withdrew. Made redundant on his twenty-first birthday. Lost his job, then lost his nerve it seems.
And so he stayed inside for hours and days and weeks until it occurred to him.
Afterwards we found that wee box they give you with the new sets. It was in his room. Well worn with his fingers. Remote control. I think they call it. I think they're right.

SCENE SIXTEEN

The club. TOMMY *joins* KITTY. DAVEY *is behind the bar.*

TOMMY: Well, whaddya hear, whaddya say?

KITTY: Well, hello, big boy, how's tricks?

TOMMY: I dunno, I ain't seen her for weeks.

KITTY: Thought I wouldn't show, huh?

TOMMY: I wasn't sure. I knew you was one class dame.

KITTY: But then you must know so many.

TOMMY: A few. I ain't met nobody like you before.

KITTY: Nor will again.

TOMMY: Fancy talker, huh?

KITTY: You ain't seen nuthin' yet.

TOMMY: What's it take to see sumthin'?

KITTY: Well, it'll certainly take a drink from that little blue-eyed barman.

DAVEY: Me?

KITTY: That's right, honey.

TOMMY: You heard what the lady said, now move those two rickety pins over here now. And when I say now I mean yesterday.

DAVEY: I wasn't workin' here yesterday.

KITTY: Don't confuse the gentleman.

TOMMY: OK, Matt, I'll have two fingers of Bourbon and a shot of red-eye for the broad.

DAVEY: The Bourbon don't come in fingers, it comes in bottles and there's no way I'm hitting the dame.

TOMMY: Now listen here, wise guy.

KITTY: I give up..I give up. I can't keep the bloody thing goin'.

TOMMY: You were doin' great. Just like Jean Harlow in the movie.

DAVEY: Ay, it wasn't bad, you know.

TOMMY: Whaddya know. You haven't even seen the picture.

DAVEY: Ay, cos you won't let me. You expect me to join in and I don't know what the hell I'm supposed to do.

TOMMY: Leave it to me. I'll explain it all in good time.

KITTY: And talkin' of time, I'll have that drink now.

TOMMY: Good idea.

KITTY: Half of lager, please.

TOMMY: Same again, Dave, and one for yourself.

DAVEY: That's big of you, Tom. You don't want to discuss money, I suppose.

TOMMY: Davey. Not in front of the lady.

DAVEY: Oh, understood, Tom. Leave it to me.

TOMMY: That shmuck. I taught him everything I know –

KITTY: And he knows nothin'.

TOMMY: Christ, you're quicker at this than I am.

TOMMY: Sort of.

KITTY: You're a spacer, mister.

TOMMY: I don't think I am and neither do you.

KITTY: No, I don't. I don't know what I think. I don't know what I'm doing here.

TOMMY: Havin' a laugh. But then you're not allowed to do that when you're out of work.

KITTY: All right. All right.

TOMMY: How's your oul fella?

KITTY: Not too great. He's gone into the hospital the day for a week or so.

TOMMY: Well, try not to worry.

KITTY: You may as well say try not to breathe.

TOMMY: Ay, point taken. Still you can always forget for a bit. That's what I do.

KITTY: Is that what it is? Forgettin' for a bit? Is that all?

TOMMY: That's all you need to know.

KITTY: I don't need to know anything about you, mister.

TOMMY: Ay, you don't need to, but do you want to?

KITTY: I like forgettin' with you.

TOMMY: Good. Are you visitin' your da tonight?

KITTY: Yeh.

TOMMY: Good. Come straight down here afterwards and we can forget together. You and me and Davey. We're all in the number.

KITTY: More performin'?

TOMMY: You're a natural. It's all in the films. It's meant to happen.

KITTY: Visitin' stops at eight.

TOMMY: Perfect. Come here. We'll do the show and afterwards. . .

KITTY: What?

TOMMY: Well, you'll be on your own in that house, won't you?

KITTY: Don't make assumptions.

TOMMY: I'll walk you home, that's all. Nothin' else. I'm not trying anything . . . I'm not.

KITTY: *I'm* sorry. Sometimes I'm too quick.

TOMMY: You're very young to be that way.

KITTY: I'm very scared.

TOMMY: Why?

(*Pause.*)

KITTY: Because I really like you, mister, and I don't think this should be happenin' this quick and –

TOMMY: I'm scared too.

KITTY: I know. I can feel that. I like that. But it's all right, isn't it? I mean, you're all right, aren't you?

TOMMY: I get depressed sometimes. 'Why, sometimes I feel lower than a whale's foot.'

KITTY: Whales don't have feet.

TOMMY: Well, next time you just look.

KITTY: That's gotta be from a movie.

TOMMY: Yeh – *Something to Sing About*.

KITTY: Is that your favourite?

TOMMY: Nah. Nobody tops Tommy Powers.

KITTY: Tommy Powers?

TOMMY: The Cagney part in *Public Enemy* – his greatest movie.

KITTY: Well, I'm gonna have to see it, aren't I?

TOMMY: I could bring it round tonight. Have you got a video?

KITTY: Yeh. OK then. Maybe see you later down here. That was a laugh earlier on.

TOMMY: We're gonna have a lot of laughs. Me, you and Davey. Ain't that right, Dave?

DAVEY: Sure thing, boss.

KITTY: Well, see you later.

TOMMY: You goin' shoppin'?

KITTY: Yeh, why?

TOMMY: Buy some grapefruit.

KITTY: What for?

TOMMY: You'll know when you've seen the film.

(*Exit Kitty.*)

The broad might be trouble, kid. Take it easy. No sweat. No strain.

The club.

DAVEY: That's the first sign of madness, talkin' to yourself. How d'ya get on with the chick?

TOMMY: Like a dream, Matt. I got that broad eatin' out of my hand. You just watch. We're gonna be like sugar candy before you can say Edward G. Robinson. So what about Pearson?

DAVEY: Yeh, what about him?

TOMMY: So where is he, Matt? I thought you'd fixed up a meet?

DAVEY: He'll come if he feels like it and for no other reason. He's a lazy git.

TOMMY: He's *gotta* show, Dave. We're movin' tonight.
(*Enter* PEARSON.)

PEARSON: Why, you dirty rat!

TOMMY: Ha, Geordie. How's yourself?

PEARSON: Not bad, you cheeky git. And it's Sergeant Pearson to you.

TOMMY: Oh, ay. Christ, I know that, Geordie. Just keepin' it hush-hush, you know. I mean, you never know who might be listenin'.

PEARSON: I couldn't give a toss who listens. They'd be dead men if they started messin' with me and the organization.

TOMMY: Right enough, mate.

PEARSON: I'm not your mate.

DAVEY: Do you wanna drink, Geordie?

PEARSON: Ay. Very civil of you, David. How's that wee brother of mine these days? Still as quiet as ever?

DAVEY: Och, ay. Sure, he wouldn't say boo to anyone. He's on this afternoon if you wanna stop and have a chat with him.

PEARSON: No. No. Just makin' sure he's not steppin' out of line. One black sheep in the family's enough, eh?

DAVEY: Ay, right.

TOMMY: Look, Geordie. About last night. I hope I didn't embarrass you there. I was just desperate to win, you know. It meant a hell of a lot to the old dear. Hope you can appreciate that.

PEARSON: Ay, sure, your old man was a cocky bastard, too. Never saw eye to eye with him, either.

THOMPSON: Only you wouldn't have said so, Geordie, would you? Not to Roy Black.

TOMMY: Ay, well, to each his own, eh?

PEARSON: Bollocks. Don't do it again, right? That contest was my idea and I run it, right?

TOMMY: No problem, Geordie.

THOMPSON: But there were a few problems weren't there, Tommy? Like your old man's death. Remember seein' him go back into that house? Still ablaze. While Pearson's mob was up the street burnin' out the rest of the Catholics. It was your oul fella tryin' to save the little old woman with her rosaries cryin' for help in that inferno. But he wasn't quick enough. For her or for him. Before the whole place collapsed on both. You remember that all right. And so does Pearson.

PEARSON: There's a few fellas wouldn't mind callin' round for a wee recruitment chat, you know. We haven't forgotten that you've avoided the call.

TOMMY: Christ, Geordie, I've got my ma to look after.

PEARSON: Thought you'd a brother.

TOMMY: Ay, we're both on the brew.

PEARSON: Then you've got time on your hands.

DAVEY: I was surprised at you doin' the talent contest, George. I hear the Army's on the prowl again. Spot checks. House searches. You need to be careful.

PEARSON: The British Army? Don't make me laugh.

TOMMY: You'd need to be a few steps ahead.

PEARSON: Well, I'm more than a few steps ahead, sunshine.

TOMMY: Must be complicated.

PEARSON: There's more to thick Irishmen than meets the eye, fella. See that wee brother of mine. How would you describe him? Ever been in trouble?

DAVEY: No way. I can vouch for that. Sure everybody knows you and him's fallen out over the UDA loads of times. He's as quiet as a mouse.

PEARSON: Right. But he's still family and he still knows when to do a favour. Have a look under his bed next time you're round there.

DAVEY: Under his bed? Why?

PEARSON: Wise up.

TOMMY: You mean . . . ?

PEARSON: He's doin' some mindin' for me and the boys. Who'd look twice at the wee lamb? Just as well, eh? Right, I'm off to see if that oul bitch has got the dinner on. You keep your nose clean, Black. Don't annoy me, right?

TOMMY: You're the boss, Paddy.

PEARSON: Cut that crap.

TOMMY: It's just a bloke from the films, that's all.

PEARSON: Ay, and I'm just a bloke from real life with a boot that could kick your arse from here to Bangor. Do you read me?

TOMMY: Over and out.

PEARSON: By the way, David, I want this place cleared by ten tonight.

DAVEY: Well, we've got the bowlin' do, George.

PEARSON: Ay, well, they'll need to be out by ten. I've got some boys comin' in here who don't want to be disturbed. So just do it, right? Regards to my brother.

DAVEY: Christ, everything stops for the mobs in this town.

TOMMY: That's right, Matt, and that dirty no-good meathead's got everything that's coming to him.

DAVEY: Now, you stop that now. Forget fellas like him. You and me and that wee girl have started having a laugh so let's keep it simple. He's a dangerous man. We'll keep well away from him and his guns – Christ, did you hear that about his brother?

TOMMY: I know, it'll be a piece of cake.

DAVEY: What?

TOMMY: You said yourself his brother's working – all I have to do is –

DAVEY: – is *nothing*, absolutely nothing, Tommy. It's too dangerous, right. Pictures or no pictures.

TOMMY: OK, Matt, OK. But we gotta change things round here.

The club. MA *joins* TOMMY *and* DAVEY.

MA: Tommy, Tommy, why didn't one of yous give me a shout?

TOMMY: What are you talking about? It's all right. It's all right. Calm down.

MA: This morning, why didn't you do something when you saw I wasn't –

TOMMY: Ma, just calm down a wee minute and tell me what it is you're on about.

MA: Simpson. He wouldn't listen. It's not as if I do it all the time.

TOMMY: What are you saying, Ma?

MA: I slept through the alarm. It must've been all the excitement of last night.

TOMMY: What, you mean you were late for work? For goodness' sake, what are you getting yourself into a state for?

MA: Cos he's sacked me, Tommy. On the spot.

TOMMY: *What?*

MA: He said he was within his rights. I hadn't a leg to stand on.

TOMMY: Why that no-good son of a –

MA: Not now, Tommy, please.

DAVEY: Here, have a wee brandy, Mrs Black.

MA: Thanks, son. Ach. I'm sorry to make a fuss. It was that much of a shock. I just don't know what we're going to do.

TOMMY: That's some repayment, isn't it, for all those years you've put in at that bloody shop?

MA: Oh, God, what are we going to do?

TOMMY: Don't worry, Ma. We'll fix something, me and Jimmy.
(*Enter* ROBERT.)

ROBERT: Oh, you're here. Good. I want a word with you – Ma, what are you doing in here?

MA: Don't be angry, son.

TOMMY: Simpson's give her the push. She slept in this morning.

ROBERT: Well, that about takes the biscuit, doesn't it?

TOMMY: Yeh, it's tough. So let's think of Ma for a change.

ROBERT: Don't tell me about looking after Ma.

27

DAVEY: Fellas, it's more than my job's worth if you start an argy in here. Look, your mother's very upset.

TOMMY: Seeing you walking round like a schoolboy can't help. Some part-time job.

ROBERT: Oh, you're too good for a paper-round, are you?

TOMMY: I thought you were on the dole, Robert. That and the car-cleaning, eh? They'd be interested to hear about that.

ROBERT: Oh, and you'd be the one to tell them, wouldn't you?

TOMMY: Only I'm not as self-righteous as you.

ROBERT: You've got some face, haven't you? The one night our ma goes out gallivantin' —

MA: I wasn't gallivantin'.

ROBERT: Chasing after your bloody stupid antics. And you plying her with drinks that she'd paid for —

TOMMY: Watch it.

ROBERT: That just happens to be the time when she manages to sleep in. Hardly surprising when you think how tired she must be. Lifting and laying you half her life.

TOMMY: Change the record.

ROBERT: I don't need to. It changes itself. I've just been trying to get the money for a paper bill from Brian Best. Remember him, your local friendly video-shop owner. Well, he's not so bloody friendly any more, I can tell you. Cos you owe him that much bloody money that I'll be paying for it before he pays for his papers — are there no other lives you can disrupt?

TOMMY: Ach, you see everything, don't you? We'll have to christen you Saint Bob.

DAVEY: That's enough. Your mother sittin' there in tears and you're rowing away in public. Get the hell skates out of here.

ROBERT: I don't have to be asked, David. I've had enough of this sponger. C'mon, mother.

TOMMY: Hey, paper-boy! Don't forget to come tonight.

ROBERT: You serious?

TOMMY: You promised you'd be there.

ROBERT: Yeh, I'll be there all right. Make sure that £20 gets straight back to Ma.

TOMMY: Just be there, Bobby.

The club. TOMMY *and* DAVEY.

DAVEY: Jesus. You've built up a fan club since you rejoined the human race.

TOMMY: It's gotta be, Matt. Bobbo's one of the lambs.

DAVEY: Hey, listen –

TOMMY: It's too late. It's all set up. We start tonight. I can't let Jimmy down. Remember kid, the dough starts rollin' in this evening. Fifty–fifty, you and me. I know that's only ten bucks apiece, but it's a start.

DAVEY: I thought that money was going to your old dear. Well, it has to now, doesn't it?

TOMMY: Listen, Dave. We're gonna look after ma better than she ever was in this town. She's gonna have everything. Peace of mind, Dave, that's what we need, not just bucks.

DAVEY: You amaze me the way you keep this up. You're a case, Tom.

TOMMY: I'm keeping it up cos it'll keep me sane.

DAVEY: You really mean that.

TOMMY: I know where I'm goin' now, Dave. And I ain't goin' nowhere for people like Robert. Some chick sure ain't gettin' a bargain with him.

DAVEY: That's gotta be a line.

TOMMY: *Public Enemy*, the best there is. Made Cagney a star.

DAVEY: This is where Matt's from, is it?

TOMMY: Yeh, Matt Doyle. Tommy Powers's best friend.

DAVEY: Well, I'll have to see it. I mean, if it's gonna take off the way you reckon, you're gonna need your partner in the act.

TOMMY: Oh, I had you signed up long ago.

DAVEY: So when do I see the picture?

TOMMY: Soon enough, son. Soon enough. After tonight. You'll need to.

DAVEY: What?

TOMMY: Meet me in Nelson Street. Six-thirty. And come on your moped.

DAVEY: Why?

TOMMY: Cos we've got to be there by seven.

DAVEY: Where?

TOMMY: I'll tell you later on – trust me. Now we're movin'.

DAVEY: Well, it'll be pretty tight. I won't be finished here till six.

TOMMY: Davey – just do it. See you later.

SCENE TWENTY

THOMPSON: I read the papers next day. This boy knew where he
was goin' all right. You could have missed it. I suppose.
Not me.
It was Part Two. *The Wonder Increases*. Same guy. Same
place. Same movie. Different routine. All done perfectly.
The locals duly impressed. *I* was impressed. The wife was
impressed.
I tell her everything. When she'll listen.
I had another drink. And read the rest of the paper.
You never know what you might find.

SCENE TWENTY-ONE

Nelson Street. TOMMY *joins* DAVEY.

TOMMY: Davey, where's the wheels?

DAVEY: Just round the corner. You're all right.

TOMMY: We got one problem.

DAVEY: Let me guess.

TOMMY: Ten pounds, that's all. Sure, you'll get it back tonight.

DAVEY: So what do you need it for now?

TOMMY: Cos we gotta go somewhere before the gig. Tonight's
the night.

DAVEY: What? You're buyin' me a drink?

TOMMY: Soon enough, kid. Tonight we buy our very own copy
of *Public Enemy*.

DAVEY: The movie – I thought you had it.

TOMMY: I've seen it, of course. Dozens of times. But I've got to own it.

DAVEY: Why?

TOMMY: It's symbolic, isn't it?

DAVEY: I bet Cagney didn't use words like that.

TOMMY: Yeh, but I am. We have to *have* it kid. That's what Jimmy wants. Hey. We're startin' to live, Dave, right?

DAVEY: Yeh. In a bloody mystery film.

TOMMY: Everything's gonna be real clear, real soon. You ain't gonna have to work in bars for the rest of your life and I ain't hangin' round for no two-bit hand-outs no more.

DAVEY: So what are you goin' to do?

TOMMY: *We*, Davey, *we*. Yeh, old Putty-Nose is gonna have to think again when it comes to Tommy Powers and Matt Doyle.

DAVEY: By the way. I'm only gonna play in up-market places from now on. No more oul clubs.

TOMMY: We're gonna make the world sit up, Davey.

DAVEY: Ay, well, talkin' of sittin' up, Brian Best won't be sittin' up much longer if you're thinkin' of buyin' that video. All the shops will be shut. Anyway, how d'ya know he's gonna have it in stock?

TOMMY: I ordered it. Long time ago.

DAVEY: Clever wee article, aren't you?

TOMMY: But not from him.

DAVEY: Oh, I see. That's why you needed muggins with the transport. Where is it?

TOMMY: Andersonstown.

DAVEY: I don't believe this.

TOMMY: It's just a video shop, Dave. They specialize in this kind of thing.

DAVEY: I just don't believe it.

TOMMY: Look, it was one of the few places I could guarantee would supply it.

DAVEY: Well, could you not find one of the few places that wasn't slap in the middle of Republican Belfast?

TOMMY: It's a wee shop about to close. It'll be empty. It'll take five minutes.

DAVEY: Have you heard of the IRA?

TOMMY: C'mon. . .

DAVEY: You don't know who you're dealing with, for Christ's sake. And what do I do? Wait outside and get my face kicked in or come in with you and get stranded cos they've taken the bike away?

TOMMY: Wise up, for God's sake.

DAVEY: You wise up. Those fellas don't look twice.

TOMMY: Look, you know nothing. When have you been into Andytown in the last ten years?

DAVEY: Exactly. Look, if we've got a dozen Geordie Pearsons and worse, so have they and they'll smell a Prod a mile away. This fella you ordered it from. Have you given him your name?

TOMMY: A false one.

DAVEY: I hope it was St Thomas. It's the only thing that'll take them in.

TOMMY: Calm down, you oul woman. All I want is the film. All I need is £10 and for you to drop me at the shop. I'll jump off the bike. You high-tail it.

DAVEY: And how do you get away?

TOMMY: Leave that to me. Now, c'mon, we need to get a move on. Remember we got a gig tonight. Go start the wheels, I'll hitch on the running board.

DAVEY: Hey, listen, mate. Are you *sure* you're all right? Inside, I mean? I worry about you, you oul bugger, you know.

TOMMY: I'm top of the world, Matt. Now start the motor.

DAVEY: I wish you'd told me. This thing needs a new clutch. (*Exit* DAVEY.)

TOMMY: Don't think about it, Dave. I do the thinking. Nice kid, Davey. But stupid. Really stupid. So. Got the wheels. Got the alibi. Now let's get moving.

SCENE TWENTY-TWO

THOMPSON: I found it in the stop press.
Too late for a proper report.

It was normal for this town.
But not for me.
I smelt something different.
Something wrong.
I knew this was it.
What was coming. Changing.
Nothing to do now, but wait.
Sometimes that's not a good idea.

SCENE TWENTY-THREE

A video shop in Andersonstown. O'DONNELL *is serving.* TOMMY
enters.

O'DONNELL: We're just closing.

TOMMY: I won't take up two minutes of your time.

O'DONNELL: Ay, well, lock the door behind you. I don't want
the rest of the town to think we're still open. What can I do
for you? Do I know you? You're not a regular in here.

TOMMY: No. I'm not. I just heard you were the best.

O'DONNELL: Ay, for some things certainly. I take it you're after
one of the gangster flicks.

TOMMY: That's right. I rang up in fact. You may remember me,
to place an order.

O'DONNELL: And what would your name be, son?

TOMMY: Powers.

O'DONNELL: Ah! Couldn't be better for the one you're after.
Public Enemy, that's right, isn't it?

TOMMY: That's it, yeh.

O'DONNELL: Same name as your man in the picture.

TOMMY: Ay. I've got a wee bit of a thing about him, you know. I
just thought I've got to have it.

O'DONNELL: Ay, well, it's one of the best. No question. Mind
you, I think I prefer him as Cody Jarrett in *White Heat* – you
know, 'top of the world' and all that.

TOMMY: Ay, that's a great favourite too. Has the tape come in,
then?

33

O'DONNELL: Oh, ay. I've got it here, son. You seem a bit
nervous. You're not from round here at all, are you?

TOMMY: No, I just want the tape, mister.

O'DONNELL: Watch yourself on the way home, son.

TOMMY: Right. How much?

O'DONNELL: Twenty-two pounds ninety-nine.
(*Pause.*)
Twenty-two pounds ninety nine.
(TOMMY *thinks, then decides.*)

TOMMY: You never said that was the price.

O'DONNELL: That's exactly what I said on the phone, son.

TOMMY: No. You never came up with that you double-crossin'
mutt. Say I only got twenty bucks?

O'DONNELL: Well then, you can't have the tape, son. You come
up with the right money and it's all yours.

TOMMY: OK, mister, forget it. (*Points the gun in his pocket at*
O'DONNELL.) Stick 'em up.

O'DONNELL: Ah. The old trick from *Angels with Dirty Faces*, eh?
Hand in pocket, pretend to be a gun. Very funny. Now,
grow up, kid, for God's sake, and don't waste my time.
(TOMMY *pulls out the gun.*)

TOMMY: Don't waste my time, shmuck. Gimme the movie.

O'DONNELL: Listen, son, don't be foolish. I've got some very
important friends round here.

TOMMY: That's exactly what I'm countin' on, sucker.
(*He shoots* O'DONNELL.)

SCENE TWENTY-FOUR

THOMPSON: And that's where I came in.
Too early.
For him.
And me.

SCENE TWENTY-FIVE

A rooftop.

TOMMY: Made it, Ma! Top of the world!

END OF ACT ONE

ACT TWO

The club. TOMMY, DAVEY *and* KITTY *are in mid-act.*

TOMMY: (*Sings:*) Give my regards to Broadway,
    Remember me to Herald Square,
    Tell all the gang on 42nd Street,
    That I will soon be there.
    Whisper of how I'm yearning,
    To mingle with the old time throng,
    Give my regards to Old Broadway
    And say that I'll be there ere long.
    (*The music continues and there is a dumb show between* DAVEY,
KITTY *and* TOMMY *throughout the next scene.*)

SCENE TWENTY-SEVEN

The club.

THOMPSON: 'Motiveless Killing'.
    That's what the stop press said.
    Beautifully planned.
    End of the day. No one about. Maximum amount in the
    till.
    And a vanishing act under the cover of darkness.
KITTY: (*To* TOMMY) Don't worry, we still believe in you,
    Johnny.
THOMPSON: Then the questions started.

    The shop was slap in the middle of Provo land.
    That kind of thing doesn't happen.
    The boys won't let it happen.

    O'Donnell himself?
    Family man. So-so business.

36

A hundred and thirty-two pounds in the till.
That don't buy you out of a life sentence.

So who'd do it? Who'd go for a little guy gettin' by in his
own part of town?
The UDA? If so, they knew something I didn't.
They wouldn't put the top fellas on this one. It was
political suicide.
It didn't make sense.

DAVEY: I want you to watch for the sky-rocket. If that goes up
you'll know I've obtained certain papers to prove you
innocent of throwing the English Derby. Remember, watch
for the sky-rocket.

TOMMY: Thanks, pal. I'll be watchin'.

THOMPSON: The call came soon enough.
'Right, Thompson, you're an old-fashioned copper, solve
an old-fashioned crime – and leave the real world to us.'
That was the gist of it.

The wife didn't say a thing.
Probably knew before I did.
This one was mine all right.

Where to start?
The oul lags file – look for inspiration.
But first I had another look at the paper.
Reminded myself of what was possible.

Same country, same city, practically the same time of day
and *two* fellas. One with some sort of new-found purpose
and the other one with that gun who . . .
I didn't know what was happening to our kids.

Kids?
What made me say that?
Maybe the old instinct was working.
But not quickly enough for Mrs O'Donnell.

(TOMMY *dances. Exit. Applause.*)

37

Kitty's house. KITTY *arrives home.*

KITTY: Hello – are you up there, mister?

TOMMY: Well, hello.

    (*He enters.*)

    Whaddya hear, whaddya say?

KITTY: Walkin' round the place half naked. I'm glad you've made yourself at home.

TOMMY: C'mere.

    (*They embrace passionately.*)

KITTY: Good morning, mister. Or should I say good afternoon. Boy, I feel all funny.

TOMMY: That's allowed.

KITTY: I'm glad, how's yourself?

TOMMY: Pretty good, kid. Did you get the grapefruit?

KITTY: Well, I dunn forgot, Mr Powers, sir.

TOMMY: Why of all the –

KITTY: I try remembrin' next time, sir, lordy lordy.

TOMMY: Yeh, well, maybe there won't be a next time, cos that's the kind of hairpin I am.

KITTY: I've got to keep you interested, big boy.

TOMMY: You kept me interested last night all right.

KITTY: I still don't believe what happened. That you're here. I've never done that before. Just kind of fallen into –

TOMMY: How old are you, kid?

KITTY: Nineteen.

TOMMY: You been with a lot of guys?

KITTY: None of your business.

TOMMY: Don't gimme no sugar-lip stuff.

KITTY: I haven't done this before if that's what you mean. Let a stranger into my life. My bed. (*Pause.*) What's inside you, mister?

TOMMY: What do you mean?

KITTY: Last night, it was more than just lust or love or whatever. I could feel something really strong inside you. Something on fire.

38

TOMMY: Excitin' eh?

KITTY: Dangerous, maybe.

TOMMY: Let's stick to excitin'. Which is just what the paper should be. Have you read the review?

KITTY: Oh, I didn't see it. I was readin' about that murder up the town last night.

TOMMY: So I'm pushed off the front page?

KITTY: You should read it. It's not much to joke about.

TOMMY: Since when's murder news in this town?

KITTY: They don't think it was the paramilitaries.

TOMMY: So the butler did it.

KITTY: It could've been anybody. By the way, where were you last night?

TOMMY: Christ. It's in the bloody paper where I was.

KITTY: I mean before that.

TOMMY: Rehearsing the bloody thing. It doesn't do itself, you know.

KITTY: You're not involved in anything, are you?

TOMMY: Like what?

KITTY: You know what I mean.

TOMMY: What do you mean?

KITTY: Organizations.

TOMMY: Yeh. I've plenty of time for that when I'm learnin' *Yankee Doodle Dandy*.

KITTY: I only asked.

TOMMY: Yeh, and that's all right, isn't it, cos you have to understand I'm a bit suspicious, cos you're a wee bit eccentric and not to be trusted and you are out of work and Christ! Is there anyone in this town ready to give you a break? I've spent my life stayin' *away* from those bastards and tryin' to keep some self-respect together in a town where they don't let you breathe and hardly anybody else gives you credit for a bit of sense, or. . .

KITTY: I'm sorry. I'm sorry.

TOMMY: It doesn't matter.

KITTY: It does. It does. Look, I do understand. I do. And I know you're angrier inside than you let on. But I just feel a bit insecure. I hardly know you, mister, but I do care for you.

I'm just a frightened wee girl sometimes, you know. You shouldn't pay any attention.

TOMMY: I'm sorry to shout. Just don't be like my brother, that's all, and the other. . . Anyway, don't worry, kid. I'm gettin' even.

KITTY: What do you mean?

TOMMY: I better be goin'.

KITTY: Do you wanna go to the pictures tonight?

TOMMY: No, not tonight. It's the homecoming tonight.

KITTY: What?

TOMMY: *Public Enemy*. It's where the brother comes home from the war and Tommy lays on a real spread and spoils his mum and stuff. I thought I'd get her some flowers. Buy Robert a few cigars.

KITTY: I didn't know Robert had been away at war.

TOMMY: He hasn't. He's just been for a job interview. It's practically the same thing. Poor sod. Must be his two hundredth. The man's a hero.

KITTY: I think he might be.

TOMMY: I know it and tonight he gets a hero's welcome, just like on the film. See you around, kid.

KITTY: He won't like it.

TOMMY: What?

KITTY: Whatever you got planned. He won't like it.

TOMMY: How come you know so much?

KITTY: I've seen the film. I watched it this morning while you were asleep.

(*Pause*.)

TOMMY: Well, Tommy Black's gonna put Tommy Powers right and . . . and . . . what do you know? You don't know nuthin'. Next time buy the grapefruit.

SCENE TWENTY-NINE

THOMPSON: Went fishin' in O'Donnell's neck of the woods. Gauge the atmosphere.

Apparently the estate he lived in was so far behind with

their rents that even the IRA decided something had to be done. So they went round gatherin' 'donations' from local businesses and handed out the various amounts to the tenants so that when the rent man arrived their books could be marked up to date.

Well, the rentman, of course, was staggered when the cash came his way on his weekly visit. Until of course he'd finished his round. That's when the boys intercepted him and reclaimed their donations.

The rentman went on his way unharmed and empty-handed, the money was returned to the donors and the rent books were all marked up to date.

That's a nice wee system those boys had goin' and Kevin O'Donnell knew it well. He was payin' the same fellas protection money every week of the year.

Not surprisingly those boys couldn't put up with the death of one of their subscribers.

Not good for business. One with a reputation to sustain. Whoever killed Kevin O'Donnell should have checked who his friends were.

Maybe they did?

Whatever, they now had the police *and* the IRA big boys on their back.

Whoever it was, I hoped I could get to him first.

SCENE THIRTY

The Blacks' house. TOMMY *joins* MA.

TOMMY: Whaddya hear, whaddya say?

MA: Oh, my good God. Where in the name of God were you last night? You know there was trouble?

TOMMY: Ay, Ma, and you know where, don't you? For goodness' sake, I'm not gonna be wandering round Andersonstown. I'm all right, stop worryin'.

MA: Stop worryin', he says. I've no job and you stay out all night

41

when there's a murderer on the loose and he says stop worryin'.

TOMMY: Ma. It was in Provo land, I told you. And it's a wee bit late to start worryin' about the paramilitaries now.

MA: They say it was nothin' to do with the paramilitaries – there's a maniac on the loose.

TOMMY: What's the difference?

MA: Never you mind what the difference is, just do as you're told and stay out of trouble. Now, where the hell were you last night?

TOMMY: If you'd read the paper you'd have seen. Do you not remember? I was dancin' away in the hall. I wish you'd been there.

MA: Yesterday was no day for celebration.

TOMMY: I know, Ma. I'm sorry about the job. But we ain't lettin' that shmuck Simpson get the better of you cos –

MA: I wasn't talking about your show. I was talking about afterwards when you had your mother up half the night.

TOMMY: I'm sorry, Ma. Look, I went round to that wee girl's.

MA: Which wee girl?

TOMMY: The one who was in the talent contest. The Country-and-Western one.

MA: Oh, ay. She was good.

TOMMY: Ay, she was. She is. She's very nice. You'd like her. Anyway, I went round there and we just got talking and before you knew what –

MA: Don't tell me.

TOMMY: Before you knew what the time was it was too late to start wanderin' the streets of Belfast. I knew you wouldn't want that.

MA: Oh, I'm sure you were thinkin' of me.

TOMMY: I was, but I couldn't get a message to you. I'm sorry. I thought you might be upset. So I brought you these.
(*He gives her a huge bunch of flowers.*)

MA: Ach, you big fool, you.

TOMMY: I got lots more surprises. Give me a hand with this.
(*They lift a huge barrel of beer on to the table.*)

MA: What the hell's this?

TOMMY: Surprise for Bob. We're gonna drink all night.
(*They hug.*)
What's that smell?
MA: Whiskey. I made a wee dent in your bottle. Calm my nerves,
son. I'll get you another one.
TOMMY: I don't need another bottle, just make sure you
don't. . . be careful, Ma . . . that's all . . . ach, drink
whatever you like. Here and forget about losin' your job.
Here's a few bob to keep you goin'.
MA: Where did this come from? Sure, Robert brought home the
money you got for the show. . .

SCENE THIRTY-ONE

The Blacks' house. ROBERT *enters.*

ROBERT: Well, somebody's had some luck. What is this? Party
time?
TOMMY: Bobby! Whaddya hear, whaddya say? You bet we're
havin' a party. Sit down and have a glass of beer. Gee, we
was rootin' for you. This is the one, kid. I know you're
gonna get this job. You're gonna be top of the world. Then
it's broads and booze. You takin' over.
ROBERT: I didn't get it.
TOMMY: You don't know that. They don't tell you these things
straight away. They'll write real long letters. They're gonna
be crazy about you.
ROBERT: I didn't get the job, the man told me.
TOMMY: That jerk didn't even think about it?
ROBERT: He didn't need to think about it. I wasn't qualified
enough. Or good enough. They're goin' to use someone else.
TOMMY: But that guy's crazy. You got book learnin' and poems
and all that fancy stuff you need for good jobs. That's you,
Bobby. *I'm* the mutt.
ROBERT: Well, it's not good enough, right? End of story, right?
TOMMY: Easy kid, easy. I know you're sore. I can understand

43

that. Gee, those guys make me wanna just . . . Hey, come on, I got more surprises.

ROBERT: I'm not in the mood, Tom.

MA: Let Robert have a wee time on his own, son.

TOMMY: But look, I got these fancy cigars. They got a fancy case and stuff and. . .

ROBERT: I don't want your cigars and I don't want your play-actin'. I had enough of that last night. And I don't want you takin' the rise out of me when I try to get an honest job.

TOMMY: I wasn't doin' nothin', I just –

ROBERT: You're half the reason people aren't interested in me. I've got your stench reeking off me.

TOMMY: Hold on a –

ROBERT: Your lethargy and your apathy and now this play-actin', which doesn't take me in for one minute. Where the hell's the money come from for all this? Have you asked him that, Ma? Has he told you what he was up to last night?

TOMMY: Right, that's it. I'm out the door. I've had enough of livin' with a saint. And as a matter of interest you're an ignorant git.

MA: Tommy.

TOMMY: Play-actin', right? That's what's produced this. Play-actin'. Money. Earnings. Remember. Got that, Mr No-Hope?

ROBERT: Watch it.

TOMMY: I've got bookings, son. I've got money comin' in. Big money. And when you can earn that for preachin' to the family, I'll give up being a nutcase. And another thing . . . Ach, Jeez. Sorry, Ma. I'm sorry. I'm tryin' to do my best.

ROBERT: Gettin' these big bookings took you all night, did it?

TOMMY: Lay off!

MA: That's enough, the both of you. I've got a great old age to look forward to with yous. What your da would say I don't know. When are you going to do these turns, son?

TOMMY: Soon.

MA: Well, we'll all come and see you.

TOMMY: Not for a bit, Ma. I wanna work on it all out of the

spotlight for a bit. Then, maybe come back and do it at the
Ulster Hall or something. Fancy that?

MA: That'd be great.

TOMMY: Top of the world, huh?

MA: Top of the world.

ROBERT: Best was askin' about your money again today.

TOMMY: He'll get his money. I'll take it in today.

ROBERT: There's no point, he won't be there.

TOMMY: Why not?

ROBERT: He's shut up shop for the day.

TOMMY: Why? It's not half-day.

ROBERT: Why do you think? Have you seen the paper?

TOMMY: Yeh.

ROBERT: Well then, you can appreciate, if anything gets through
to that brain of yours, that there's a few video-shop owners
who are a wee bit nervous today.

TOMMY: That was a one-off.

ROBERT: How d'ya know?

TOMMY: Bound to be.

ROBERT: Best doesn't think so. Neither do the police.

TOMMY: What do you mean?

ROBERT: They were round to him today. They don't know where
to start, so they're checking everything. Going to all the
other shops in the city. I wouldn't be surprised if they
wanted a word in your ear.

TOMMY: What the hell for?

ROBERT: Well, you were in there often enough spendin' Ma's
money on films.

TOMMY: So what's that got to do with anything?

ROBERT: You tell me.

SCENE THIRTY-TWO

The Blacks' house. Enter DAVEY.

DAVEY: Tommy – oh sorry. Sorry, Mrs Black, Robert. I didn't
know you were here. I was after Tommy.

45

TOMMY: I'm here, Davey. Whaddya hear, whaddya say?

MA: Are you all right, son?

DAVEY: Ay, I'm fine. Just a bit out of breath, you know.

ROBERT: Somethin' botherin' you, Davey?

DAVEY: No. I'm fine. I'm fine. I just dropped in for a bit of crack with Tom. Are you comin'?

MA: Stay where yous are. I'm away to lie down. I'd precious little sleep last night.

DAVEY: All the best then, Mrs Black.

TOMMY: Night, Ma.

ROBERT: I'm right behind you, Ma. I'll bring you a cup of tea in the mornin', OK?

MA: All right, son.

ROBERT: Good night, David.

DAVEY: Night, Bob.

(*Exit* ROBERT *and* MA.)

TOMMY: Gee, Dave, you sure were burnin' some gas back there. I thought –

DAVEY: Just tell me it's not true, Tommy. Please just say it's not true. You didn't do it. Tell me you left before it happened. Cut the crap. Just tell me you were round at the bird's – anything. Just, please God, tell me it wasn't you, please, Tommy.

TOMMY: I had to, kid.

DAVEY: Oh no. Oh Jesus, God, no. No, Tommy, no. Please, God, no. What are we gonna do? Tommy, Tommy, you bastard. You stupid bastard. I knew it. I knew it. Oh, God, what's gonna happen?

TOMMY: Easy kid. There ain't nuthin' to get heated up about, see? It was a clean job. No sweat. No strain. Just like in the movies.

DAVEY: Well, this isn't the movies, for Christ's sake! It's real life and that poor sod's dead and there's nothin' but mess and I'm scared to death. I don't wanna die, Tommy, and I don't want to go to prison. I'm havin' nothin' more to do with this, understand?

TOMMY: That's it, kid, get it all out. Give it your best shot, let it out, let it out.

46

DAVEY: Shut up!

TOMMY: Sure, kid, sure. Now listen, kid, and listen good. Get this straight. Last night a two-bit bum who crossed Tommy Powers bit the dust. End of story, right? Cops don't know nothin'. They can't figure it out in this town. We're in the clear. There's nothin' that can lead them to you or me. It was late. There was no one around and when people hear a shot in this town they don't bat an eyelid. Believe me, kid. I got this thing wrapped up so tight, no one's gonna know nothin'.

DAVEY: Tommy. Tommy. Speak to me. *What are* you doing?

TOMMY: It's gonna be all right. No one knows anything. Don't worry. Just lie low for a bit.

DAVEY: Christ. What do you think I gonna do? Put an ad in the paper saying I'm involved?

TOMMY: Lie low for a bit and just act as if normal.

DAVEY: Jeez, Tommy, you're cool about this, aren't you? I don't know what frightens me more. Being found out or you.

TOMMY: Look. What did you do? You've done nothing. You're not involved. Don't worry.

DAVEY: What a thing to say. 'Don't worry.'

TOMMY: It'll get you nowhere. Leave it to me. I've got things in hand.

DAVEY: Oh, Tommy, Tommy, Tommy.

TOMMY: C'mon. Cup of tea. Then we'll sit you down in front of the TV and you can see how it's all meant to happen.

SCENE THIRTY-THREE

THOMPSON: The town was startin' to bubble.
And so were our labs.
The bullet that took out O'Donnell.
Interesting history, the boys told us.
Fired from a gun that had seen a lot of action.
UDA hard boys on the rampage.

But this job wasn't like them.
It couldn't be. What for?

47

So *who* used it? And who had it?

Questions I was keen to answer.

And, believe me, so were the UDA.

Find that gun and we had every chance of nailing some of the hardest bastards in this town.

And didn't they just know it.

The race was on.

A three-horse race. The IRA, the UDA, and the police.

That must be a record. Whoever it was had killed the wrong guy with the wrong gun. All for £130.

If he'd known that he wouldn't have started.

Unless that's what he wanted?

I'd given up lookin' for logic.

I saw a guy rattlin' the mobs.

And a way to nail some evil for good.

If I played it right. And made this one work *for* me.

There was little to go on.

We checked O'Donnell's files.

Erratic records, but we checked his membership list.

Nothing.

He did keep a note of new orders.

The last of which was for a film called *Public Enemy*.

Life's full of wonderful ironies, isn't it?

SCENE THIRTY-FOUR

Nelson Street. PEARSON *and* DAVEY *meet.*

PEARSON: Davey! What 'bout you?

DAVEY: Not, er – not so bad, Geordie. How's yourself?

PEARSON: Oh, I'm all right.

DAVEY: Well, anyway, Geordie. I've got to make tracks. I'm late for work.

PEARSON: Have you got a light, son?

DAVEY: Yeh. Here you are. Look, I've really got to be – Oh,

Christ, Geordie, what are you doing? Aagh!

(*He is pinned against the wall.*)

Ah, for God's sake, Geordie, what have I done? Let me go please.

PEARSON: Where's your mate?

DAVEY: Who do you mean?

(PEARSON *twists his arm again.*)

Aagh. Oh, Christ, you'll break my arm.

PEARSON: Where's your mate, Jimmy bloody Cagney?

DAVEY: I don't know, Geordie. I haven't seen him. Honest to God, I don't know where he is.

PEARSON: See this lighter?

(*He puts it under* DAVEY's *bottom.*)

DAVEY: What are you doin', Geordie? You'll set my arse on fire.

PEARSON: Shut your mouth.

DAVEY: Ach, switch it off, Geordie.

PEARSON: Shut your mouth and listen. You get to that wee bastard as quick as your legs'll carry you and you give him a message from me. You tell him we don't think it was the tooth fairy took those guns, right. And we don't think the man in Andersonstown committed suicide, right.

DAVEY: Right, right, right. Switch it off, Geordie, please.

PEARSON: So your film-star mate's way out of line, right? He's a cocky wee bastard, I know. Well, you let him know that he's upset some very important men. Very violent men. They want that gun back before it lands them in trouble. Cos then they'll be angry. And that's not nice to see. Now I'm not too popular, cos I was supposed to be looking after it, right? That makes my life a bit uncomfortable and if it doesn't come back pronto, yours is gonna be more than uncomfortable. Understand what I mean? Now do yourself a favour and get that bastard. Tell him we're after him and he'd better let us get to him before the cops do. Do you read me?

(*He knees* DAVEY *in the groin.*)

DAVEY: Yes, yes, yes. Don't hit me any more.

PEARSON: Get a move on while you can still move.

(PEARSON *exits.*)

DAVEY: Oh, Jesus, Jesus, God.

SCENE THIRTY-FIVE

THOMPSON: The mobs were very annoyed.
Both sides, so my spies told me.
'What sort of protection racket is this?' they cried to the
Provos.

And the UDA knew they had a nutcase with a Christmas
box for the cops.
Neither side were getting anywhere, but nervous.

And so was I.
One lead.
We'd checked every video shop in the city.
Brian Best.
A shop in the Protestant heartland had hired out every
Cagney movie there was to one T. Black. It had to be the
guy I'd read about in the papers.

A hunch. But it could have been somethin'.
We couldn't find *Public Enemy* in O'Donnell's shop.
I had an excuse to make inquiries with Black. The boy was
way behind with payments to Best.

I had to talk to a few people.

Before someone else did.

SCENE THIRTY-SIX

The Blacks' house. THOMPSON *is visiting* MA.

MA: I didn't think Brian Best would have took it this far,
Inspector.

THOMPSON: Well, he hasn't been difficult up to now. But he does have a business to run.

MA: Ay, I've heard that before.

THOMPSON: Sorry?

MA: That's what my boss told me when he gave me the sack. Drink?

THOMPSON: No, thanks. I'm sorry. This was recent? The job?

MA: Ay, that's right. Maybe I'll beat the boys' record.

THOMPSON: What?

MA: For being out of work. Unemployment. I don't know if you've noticed it about on your travels? Have you any kids of your own?

THOMPSON: Ay. Not left school just yet.

MA: Don't let them. Stop yourself worryin' into retirement.

THOMPSON: About your son. He uses the shop a lot, doesn't he?

MA: Ay.

THOMPSON: Where is he?

MA: To be perfectly honest, I don't know.

THOMPSON: Why not?

MA: My business.

THOMPSON: Mrs Black, it'd save a lot of time with this if you'd just be straight with me and stop a little problem from becoming a big problem.

MA: He's left home. Can't get on with his brother at the moment. If their father was alive he'd have taken the belt to them both.

THOMPSON: How long have you been widowed?

MA: Too long. I *think* he's gone away. He chittered something about leaving. I don't know where he is or what he's up to and I'm too old to keep caring about it. Anyway, the long and the short is, no. I don't know where he is.

THOMPSON: Well. I would like to talk to him. About a couple of things. But do tell him it's just routine, a bit of a chat, that's all. I'm sure we can sort it out with no trouble to yourself. Does he have a job at the moment?

MA: No. That's half the problem.

THOMPSON: Problem?

MA: With them all. The whole lot of them. Me now as well. No work. Nothin' in their lives. Is it something we've done? I was brought up when there was no work about, you know. I was never unhappy the way I see my kids are. Somethin' in their eyes. Somethin' lost in their eyes. I keep thinkin' – is it my fault? What would their father have said or done? What should I do? What *do* you do for kids now? They've got everything. Television, video. Most of the things we never had, but their lives are empty. Empty.

THOMPSON: Maybe you could ask your son to give me a ring. Save a lot of bother.

MA: I'll pass on the message, if I see him.

THOMPSON: Are these his tapes?

MA: That's right.

THOMPSON: Old movie buff, eh? These are all black-and-white.

MA: I don't know. Don't know what he is. I gave up takin' an interest long time ago. At least it's kept him quiet.

THOMPSON: *Public Enemy*? How long's he had this?

MA: I've no idea.

THOMPSON: How long's he been out of work?

MA: Nearly two years.

THOMPSON: Long time.

MA: I know.

THOMPSON: Thanks for your time, Mrs Black.

SCENE THIRTY-SEVEN

The Blacks' house. TOMMY *enters.*

TOMMY: What did *he* want?

MA: Will you stop creepin' up on me like that. I suppose you were round at your whoor's again?

TOMMY: She's not a 'whoor'. And what did he want?

MA: Meet the article for one night and the next day you're sharing house and home with her. That's some way to live. Well, see if she'll put up with your loafin' –

TOMMY: Ma, Ma. You shouldn't touch this stuff. You always get this way.

MA: Don't shush me. I'll get whatever the hell way I want.

52

TOMMY: Tell me what the peelers are after?

MA: Brian Best's money, that's what. What did you think?

TOMMY: Nothin'. What am I supposed to think? I come home
and the cops are interviewing my ma.

MA: There's nothin' wrong, is there? You're not hidin' anything
from me?

TOMMY: No way, Ma. Now what did I tell you – from now on top
of the world.

MA: Not for bloody me, it isn't.

TOMMY: I told ya, quit worrying.

MA: That'll be the day. Just make sure you stay out of trouble.
Pay that man and stick to all your Cagney games and
shenanigans and just stay out of trouble, right?

TOMMY: Anything for you, Ma. Why don't you go lie down, Ma?
Huh? Take it easy. I'll bring you something, right? Don't
worry. OK?
(*Exit* MA.)

SCENE THIRTY-EIGHT

The Blacks' house. Enter DAVEY.

DAVEY: Jesus Christ, Tommy –

TOMMY: What are you tryin' to do? Tell the whole
neighbourhood you're yella?

DAVEY: I'm sorry, Tommy. I'm sorry. It's just –

TOMMY: C'mon. Pull yourself together, shmuck, before I –

DAVEY: No, listen. Tommy. Listen. You've got to. The guns.
The guns you took. They weren't new. They've got
histories. The UDA. The really hard men have used them
again and again. If the cops get the gun they've got every
chance of nailin' them. Pearson's being leant on. I don't
mean by other loudmouths. By killers. Hard bastards.
Tommy, they're after you. They're after the both of us.
We've got to do something or we're dead men.

TOMMY: So the mob's makin' a move, huh?

DAVEY: Yeh, and they're not the only ones. I heard fellas talkin'

in the bar today. That video shop was in an IRA protection
racket. It had to be. They all are, for Christ's sake.

TOMMY: Well, whaddya know?

DAVEY: I'll tell you what I know. That if it is true the IRA's not
gonna let that happen again. They'll come lookin' for you,
too.

TOMMY: So the mobs got rattled, huh?

DAVEY: 'Mobs'? Tommy, we're talking the most violent men in
this town and they're after you.

TOMMY: Just mobs, Dave. Just like the movies.

DAVEY: Your head's away, mate.

TOMMY: My head's screwed on just fine, kid. I'm gettin' us out
of this, see?

DAVEY: How? Just tell me how. Look, it's gang warfare these
people understand. They get you when you're least
expecting it. In the bath. At church. They drive up behind
you in cars.

TOMMY: I know, Dave. I seen it all.

DAVEY: So what do the bloody movies tell you to do?

TOMMY: We've got to the 'sit-out', Matt. That's what we do.
Paddy Ryan'll join us. Everything's going to be as sweet as
can be, just like I planned it.

DAVEY: Tommy, wake up! You can't have planned this. What
have you got?

TOMMY: I told you I was gettin' out, Dave. There's only one
way.

DAVEY: But what have you got, mate? A hundred pound from
that fella's till. Does that get you out of Belfast? Does that
buy you a fast car? A holiday? All the things you wanted.
You haven't got them. Only trouble. You're on the run. On
the run from the mobs. On the run from the police. What
for? What have you got?

TOMMY: Don't ask, Davey.

DAVEY: I give up. Jesus.

TOMMY: Are you excited, Dave?

DAVEY: Am I *what*?

TOMMY: Excited? Exhilarated.

DAVEY: Tommy. You're not well.

TOMMY: I'm as well as I've ever been, kid. I ain't dumb. And I
     ain't mad. I'm living, Dave. And I'm changing things.
DAVEY: You've changed nothin' but the date of your funeral.
TOMMY: I ain't trying to screw you up, kid. You're in on this cos
     I love ya. You hear? I know best, OK?
DAVEY: Tommy, Tommy.
TOMMY: Dave.
DAVEY: Yeh.
TOMMY: Do you know what the weather forecast is for the next
     couple of days?
DAVEY: No, Tommy. Strangely enough. I don't.
TOMMY: Don't you think it's gonna rain?
DAVEY: I don't know. I don't know, Tommy. Maybe.
TOMMY: Good. It's gotta rain. C'mon pal. Let's get a drink.
     Somewhere *very* quiet.

SCENE THIRTY-NINE

THOMPSON: Okay, it was instinct.
     But supposin' it had been Black?
     I had nothin' on him, except a certain reported
     eccentricity and a confirmed passion for old movies.
     Why do people watch old movies?
     Obsession with the past?
     Well, that's a national sport in this country.

     But things were changin'.
     And this particular crime was something new. Dangerous.
     If it was Black, why the newspaper advertising?
     What did he want?
     And where did he get the gun?
     And what about the mobs? I smelt panic.
     I wondered how near they were.

Nelson Street. Enter DAVEY *and* TOMMY. PEARSON *is doubled up in pain.*

DAVEY: Hold on, Tom, for Christ's sake. Look who it is.

TOMMY: I think Geordie's friends have been doin' a little bendin' his ear.

DAVEY: If that's what he gets, what the hell are we due for? C'mon, let's head off. We've got to get out of this town.

TOMMY: Hold it, kid. Let's not waste a chance. Ask a few questions. Put ourselves two steps ahead of those shmucks.

DAVEY: No! Come on.

TOMMY: Hey, Geordie!

PEARSON: Oh, it's you, is it?
(*He is obviously hurt.*)

TOMMY: You're not lookin' your best, fella. Weren't expecting company? Looks like you could do with a bit of help.

PEARSON: Not from you, mate. I thought maybe I'd run into you at some stage. Pity it's too late.

TOMMY: I think it might be too late for you, sucker.

PEARSON: Least I'm standing. Don't know that you'll be able to do the same.

DAVEY: Tommy, let's go.

TOMMY: Hold on, Matt. So the boys have taken matters into their own hands, right?

PEARSON: That's right, big shot. There'll be no more requests. No more talking. You're both dead men.
(*A car approaches in the distance.*)
And if I was you I'd leave this town, while there's still a chance of not leaving it in a wooden box.

TOMMY: The trouble with you sucker is –

DAVEY: Tommy, for God's sake, look –
(*Shots ring out from the passing car.* DAVEY *and* PEARSON *are hit.* TOMMY *pulls out a gun and shoots back. The car thunders past.*)

Nelson Street.

DAVEY: Oh God, Tommy. I'm not gonna make it.

TOMMY: Sure y'are, kid. We're gonna get the doc straight to you.

DAVEY: No way, Tom. I've got a terrible pain here.

(TOMMY *tries to move him.*)

Aagh. No. No. Let me just sit here, Tom, for a wee while. Just a minute.

TOMMY: Sure, kid, sure. We gotta watch it though. This place'll soon be crawlin' with cops.

DAVEY: Tommy, *why?*

TOMMY: C'mon, kid, we gotta move.

DAVEY: *Why*, Tommy? Why did you do this to me? You knew what was gonna happen, didn't you? (*Pause.*) Didn't you?

TOMMY: Davey, I –

DAVEY: You *planned* it, didn't you?

TOMMY: Dave. . .

DAVEY: Oh, Jesus, Tommy. I didn't know that was the way it was inside you. Why didn't you tell me about it? Why didn't we talk, mate? You can't plan things like this for other people. You can't have wanted this, mate. I was all right, honest I was. I'd have helped. I'd have helped you, mate. Why didn't you ask? You're allowed to ask your mate for help. I wouldn't have hated you for it. Get out of this, Tom. Please. For me. You're not better off comin' with me, whatever you think.

TOMMY: It's too late, Davey –

DAVEY: I don't hate you, mate, right? I'm your friend, right? Friendship, that's what you've got inside you. I'm your mate, Tommy Black. You hear me? You carry that on. Carry that on with you. I'm your mate. Davey Boyd's your mate. . .

TOMMY: I'm sorry, Davey. Oh, Davey, don't die, please. Please please don't die. Davey, Davey! (*Sobs.*) This guy. This guy. (*Cagney*) C'mon shmuck. You tried to tell him. He wouldn't listen. You did him a favour. But he never did a bad thing.

Never thought of himself. Just me. And that's the way it has
to be, right? That's how Matt buys it in the film. It had to
happen. He wouldn't have understood. He's better off. He's
better off. Now get movin', kid. C'mon, c'mon. It's gotta
rain. Gotta rain. Get goin', kid. Get goin'. This is it. The big
one. Last lap. I'm givin' you power to change things in this
town. They've got nothin' here till *they* go. Till you crack the
mobs. So take the chance. For you and Davey. Top of the
world, right? (*As himself*) Right.

SCENE FORTY-TWO

THOMPSON: Why? Why? Why?

> Nice fella.
> Nice wee job in a bar.
> No connections with the mobs. No nothin'.
> Gone.
> Messy, nasty, dirty.
> What do you tell Mrs Boyd?
> Christ, what do you tell Geordie Pearson's wife even?

> It had to be Black they were after.

> *What* was his game?

> Still no sign of him and just *one* clue to how this guy might
> think.

> I made a trip to the movies.

SCENE FORTY-THREE

Kitty's house. KITTY, TOMMY. *Breakfast. Grapefruit.*

TOMMY: What's the weather forecast for today?

58

KITTY: Is that all you can say, Tommy?

TOMMY: What do you want me to do, start blubbin'?

KITTY: No . . . but . . . Why? *Why* did it happen? I just don't understand. What were you mixed up in?

TOMMY: Nothin'.

KITTY: Then why is your friend – why is he dead?

TOMMY: If I knew that I wouldn't be sittin' here.

KITTY: I can't believe this.

TOMMY: Believe it and shut up.

KITTY: Get out. You get your stuff and you get out of here.

TOMMY: Right.

KITTY: I want you out.

TOMMY: I get the message.

KITTY: It should have been you.

TOMMY: Thanks very much.

KITTY: It should have been you. You were the one they were after.

TOMMY: Who's *they*?

KITTY: Ach, come on. Your friend's dead. Your best friend and you're sittin' here trying to behave as if nothin' has happened. You must think I'm completely stupid.

TOMMY: Not completely. When you're on your back –
(*She slaps his face.*)
Feel better?

KITTY: What is *wrong* with you?

TOMMY: What the hell do you think's wrong with me? D'ya think I'm celebratin' inside? He was my mate. And if you wanna know something, I think he's better off where he is. And so are we all.

KITTY: You don't mean that?

TOMMY: Don't I? Right, you line up my prospects, sweetheart, and work out whether I'm jokin'. Work out your own, when you're at it.

KITTY: Why are you like this? Why?

TOMMY: Eighteen months, eighteen months, going on eighty years in Chicago, wise up, kid, and don't ask me about Davey. I'm sortin' it out.

KITTY: There's nothin' to sort out. You can't bring him back.
Just tell me what happened, that's all.

TOMMY: I've had enough of your jip, kid.

KITTY: I want to know what happened.

TOMMY: I ain't tellin' you twice.

KITTY: I found the gun. I found the gun you used to kill that
man.

TOMMY: You snoopin', no-good, stinkin' broad. Why don't you
just —
(*Takes grapefruit. Throws it away. Breaks plate in half. Holds
jagged edge to her throat. Stops. Throws it away.*)

KITTY: Where are you going?
(*He goes.*)
(*To herself*) Oh no . . . oh . . . no.

SCENE FORTY-FOUR

THOMPSON: Then everything happened at once.

We couldn't find Black.
Neither could the mobs.
And they both needed him badly.
So badly that the inevitable happened.

People don't believe, of course. But it goes on.
Collusion.
The big boys on either side get together. It makes sense
when you're runnin' a business.
Bugger politics.
This was a classic case for joint know-how.
And so my spies came back with the 'buzz'.
A joint meeting was being set up by the big boys.
To discuss the disposal of one T. Black.

Meanwhile, I'd seen half the movie.
We were dealin' with some fella.

What it came out of I don't know, but this was the most intricate working of a death wish I could have imagined.

The detail. The obsession.
Everything Black had done had been to live out *his* version of Tommy Powers in that absurd bloody film.
I knew what he'd done and what he planned to do.
Everything he'd set up. Everything was to bring real life to this point in the movie. *That* particular gun, that particular shop, all for this. Get the mobs on your back. Then get them together. Then . . . what?

Revenge. One chance. Revenge for Davey Boyd.
Revenge for Belfast.

Who was this guy?

I had to move fast.

SCENE FORTY-FIVE

A street. TOMMY *alone. Enter* ROBERT.

ROBERT: Tommy! Tommy!
TOMMY: Hey, big brother. Whaddya hear, whaddya say?
ROBERT: Tommy, what's going on? The police have been back.
They're lookin' all over for you. And it's not just the police.
There have been other men at the house. Evil men. Tommy,
what's going on? You've got Ma scared out of her wits.
TOMMY: Not for long, kid. She's gonna be great. Top of the
world.
ROBERT: Stop this. It's not going to work any more. Listen. That
man in the shop is dead. Geordie Pearson's dead and Davey
Boyd who never did anybody in the world any harm is dead
and you're nowhere to be seen. Now, what are you involved
in? Tell me.
TOMMY: Why should I tell you?

ROBERT: I'm your brother, for goodness' sake.

TOMMY: And what sort of brother have you been all these years, Bobbo?

ROBERT: It won't work, Tom. I'm not going to rise to it. And this isn't the time to start all that. You're in trouble and I need to know what's going on before your mother has a nervous breakdown or somebody else gets hurt.

TOMMY: But *why*, Bobby-wobby? C'mon, tell me before I go, what have you ever done, eh?

ROBERT: Tried to help you like I'm doing now. Help you. Set an example. Get you out of your usual trouble.

TOMMY: Why?

ROBERT: Cos you're my brother. How many times –

TOMMY: But you don't *like* me.

ROBERT: That's got nothin' to do with it.

TOMMY: But that's what I thought brothers were supposed to do. Like each other. Love each other. Help each other.

ROBERT: Well, like I said, that's what I'm trying to do, you ignorant git.

TOMMY: Language, Bobby.

ROBERT: Right, that's it. I'm gettin' you home.

TOMMY: No, you're not.

ROBERT: Don't make it difficult, Tommy. You're comin' home.

TOMMY: No. I'm not going home. And I *won't* be going home. Ever again. I'll never see you again, Robert. And, you know, that makes me so happy, cos, well . . . you see . . . how can I put this, Robert . . . I mean . . . I know you're my brother and everything, but the fact is I don't like you. Not one bit. In fact, I hate your guts. I've hated you ever since I can remember.

ROBERT: I don't have to listen to this.

TOMMY: Exactly. Why break the habit of a lifetime? You never thought of me having anything useful to say before. The only interest you've ever taken in me and my ma is when you think you 'ought to'. You live your life for other people, Robert. For what *they* think, what they expect, what you're 'supposed' to do. Like lookin' after some guy just cos he's your brother.

Well, some of us are fed up with what we're 'supposed' to do, especially when we're prevented from doing it, like not gettin' the job you're supposed to be entitled to.

Well, little brother here has decided to do exactly what he wants, not what he's 'supposed' to. That's the world I'm livin' in, Robert, and if I wanna kill some bloke just cos I don't like him, then I will.

ROBERT: What has *happened* to you?

TOMMY: I've woken up, Bobbo, that's what's happened. You think me and Jimmy C. live in fantasy land. Well, that's where the real world is, mate, for the likes of us. You carry on doin' work-experience schemes and doin' your paper round for tuppence a week. Not me, I'm meetin' up with Matt on the other side. We're gonna set up with Paddy Ryan – maybe get into some bootleggin'. . .

ROBERT: You're mad.

TOMMY: Not a chance, you dreamy bastard. My mind's clearer than it's ever been. No limits. No fear.

Look at yourself. You've everything to have and nothin' to live for. Use your imagination. Find a way out of Chicago.

Imagination? You haven't got one, Robert, or you'd see *where* you're livin', *how* you're livin'. You threw your imagination away when you gave up the fight and started lookin' for a job with everyone else.

ROBERT: Why you little –

(ROBERT *starts punching him repeatedly. Violently.* TOMMY *doesn't resist.*)

Little bastard. Bit of anarchy. Is that what you want? Well, here have a bit of mine. (*Kicks him.*) I wanna kill you, you little bastard, but that's all right, isn't it? You said so yourself.

TOMMY: Across the jaw, Bob. C'mon, you must've seen the picture.

ROBERT: You filthy little pervert.

(*Final assault. Exit* ROBERT.)

THOMPSON: I watched that same bit of film again and again.

It's raining. Cagney waits for them to arrive. All the real
big-time hoodlums turn up. Dangerous men. He walks in
with a machine-gun and sprays them all over the walls.
He gets hit and dies in the gutter.

All I had to do was step in early. Round 'em up.
We got the kid. We got half of mean Belfast.

But have we got it right?

Black was doin' what a lot of us wish we could do.
Should do.

How many times do you get a chance to change things?

Not many.
So, turn a blind eye.
Let the bastards shoot it out.
Black's been right up to now.

Just once. Just once.
Let me beat them at their own game.

SCENE FORTY-SEVEN

A street. Rain. The mob arrives. TOMMY *watches.*

TOMMY: Your time just run out, fellas.
    (*He takes out a machine-gun. Enter* KITTY.)
KITTY: Tommy.
TOMMY: Jesus, kid. What the hell you doin' here? You know this
    ain't the right part of town for a broad like you. They got
    people watchin' this place. Bad men.

KITTY: I know, that's why I came. I was worried about you.

TOMMY: You're one crazy broad. Now, skedaddle. Head on home and don't stop to talk to no one.

KITTY: Tommy. I'm frightened.

TOMMY: I know you're frightened. And that's why you came down here shaking and talking to me as if I'm already in the funny farm.

KITTY: I just wanted to try and –

TOMMY: Try and save me, huh? Is that it? You've seen the movie. You know what's gonna happen and now you're gonna save me. Is that right?

KITTY: Don't go through with this, Tommy.

TOMMY: Listen, kid. I don't need to be saved. They're takin' me out of this. Rocky Sullivan, Cady Jarrett, Tommy Powers. They're the guys I understand. They're tough, but they ain't evil like those sons of bitches.

KITTY: Don't go in there, Tommy.

TOMMY: There's no other way, kid. Don't worry, you're not involved. You got mixed up with me, but you're not involved. Don't worry.

KITTY: It isn't that, Tommy. I just wanna to know *why*.

TOMMY: Cos I got nuthin' else! There ain't nuthin' else this side. Those people are scum. I'm doin' right gettin' rid of them. Make this place safe for Ma. For a lot of mas.

KITTY: But what about others, Tommy?

TOMMY: I don't care about nobody. And they don't care about me. I admit it. They won't. That's the difference. I don't care about nobody 'cept Ma and Davey. I did Davey a favour. He'll know it when I see him on the other side. And Ma's OK. She's got it inside. She's got that strength. They don't give it to our generation any more.

KITTY: And what about me?

TOMMY: What about you?

KITTY: Do you care about me, mister? Please.

TOMMY: I think it's time you went home, kid.

KITTY: Please don't do this, mister.

TOMMY: Go home, kid.

KITTY: Goodbye, Tommy Black. You know what this means, don't you?

TOMMY: Sure, I know it. I want it. Now cheer up, kid. Whaddya hear, whaddya hear?

(TOMMY *enters the bar. Sound of firing. He staggers out.* KITTY *runs back to him.*)

Get out of here –

(KITTY *is caught in the fire from the bar. Falls dead.* TOMMY *staggers ahead. Falls in the gutter.*)

I ain't so tough.

SCENE FORTY-EIGHT

THOMPSON: She could have been my daughter. Would it have been worth it *then*?

Before I threw my badge in I wrote down the last caption from that film.

'The end of Tom Powers is the end of every hoodlum. The public enemy is not a man. Nor is it a character. It is a problem that sooner or later, we, the public, must solve.'

Is that right now?

Thanks for puttin' me wise.

THE END